Caillou®

At The Dentist

Text: Johanne Mercier
Illustrations: Tipéo
Coloration: Marcel Depratto

chouette

Today, Caillou is going to the dentist for the first time.
"Let's hurry, Caillou, we don't want to be late!"
Mommy calls.
Caillou doesn't answer. Where has he gone?

Mommy finds Caillou in the bathroom.
"Caillou," she chuckles, "you've already brushed
your teeth this morning!"
"Do they look nice, Mommy?"
"Yes, Caillou, they're beautiful. Now come on,
time to go!"

At the dentist's office, Caillou and Mommy sit in the
waiting room. Caillou holds Teddy very tight. Just then,
he hears a strange whirring noise.
"Teddy, you're coming with me to see the dentist,
okay?" Caillou whispers.

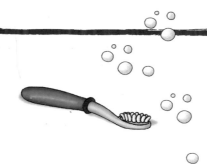

A woman with a friendly smile walks toward Caillou. "Hello, Caillou! My name is Linda. Come with me and I'll show you and your teddy the best way to brush your teeth."

Caillou and Mommy follow Linda into a small room.
There's a big chair in the middle, with a big
funny-looking lamp hanging over it.
"Have a seat, Caillou," she says.
Linda shows Caillou how the chair can move up and down.
"Can Teddy sit too?" Caillou asks her.
"Of course he can!"

Caillou and Teddy sit in the dentist's chair. Linda tilts
the back of the chair so that Caillou can lie down.
But Caillou stays sitting straight up!
"Lie back, Caillou," Linda says gently. "That way I can
get a better look at your teeth."

Linda shows Caillou the little mirror that's used to see the teeth in the back of his mouth. She starts the electric toothbrush that turns very fast.
"So that's what was making the strange noise!" Caillou tells Linda.

"Now I'm going to make your teeth shine like
little stars," Linda says.
"Okay," Caillou answers, checking first to see
if Mommy is still there.
Yes, Mommy is right behind him.

Linda brushes Caillou's teeth. Then the dentist comes into the room to give Caillou his checkup.

"Hi, Caillou, I'm Dr. Joseph. Wow, you have really nice teeth! Do you brush them every day?"

"Two times this morning!" Caillou answers proudly.

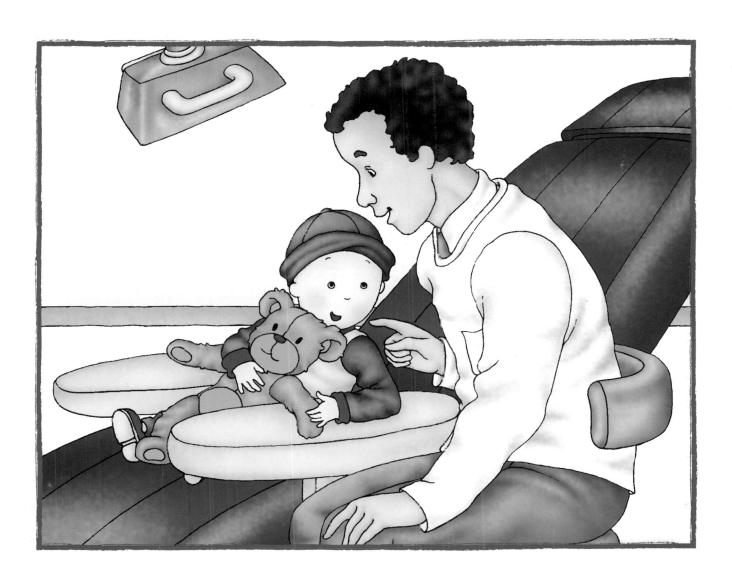

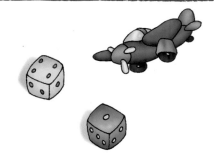

When Caillou is ready to leave, Linda gives him a new toothbrush to take home. "And you can have two surprises from the box," she tells him.
"Two?!" Caillou exclaims, examining the items in the box. He chooses a magnifying glass and a ring. "The magnifying glass is for me, and the ring is for my mommy!"

It's been a big day for Caillou. Today, he went to the dentist for the first time!

Text: Johanne Mercier
Consultant: Dr. Paule Salvail, pediatric dentist
Illustration concept: Carole Lambert
Illustrations: Tipéo
Coloration: Marcel Depratto
Art Director: Monique Dupras

We gratefully acknowledge the financial support of BPIDP and SODEC
for our publishing activities.

National Library of Canada cataloguing in publication data

Mercier, Johanne
Caillou at the dentist
(Out and About)
Translation of: Caillou chez le dentiste.
For children aged 3 and up.
ISBN 978-2-89450-497-0

1. Dental care - Juvenile literature. 2. Children - Preparation for dental care -
Juvenile literature. I. Tipéo. II. Title. III. Series: Out and About (Montreal,
Quebec).

RK63.M4713 2004   j617.6   C2003-942133-3

Legal deposit: 2004

Printed in China
10 9 8 7 6 5 4 3 2